What's Wrong with Grandma?

Spirit in the
DESERT
Retreat
Center
P.O. Box 3254
Carefree, AZ 85377

A Family's Experience with Alzheimer's

What's Wrong with Grandma?

Margaret Shawver

ILLUSTRATED BY JEFFREY K. BAGBY

Prometheus Books

59 John Glenn Drive
Amherst, New York 14228-2119

Published 2003 by Prometheus Books

Inquiries should be addressed to
Prometheus Books
59 John Glenn Drive
Amherst, New York 14228-2119
VOICE: 716–691–0133, ext. 210
FAX: 716-691-0137
WWW.PROMETHEUSBOOKS.COM

11   7 6

Originally published in hardcover

Library of Congress Cataloging-in-Publication Data

Shawver, Margaret.
    What's wrong with Grandma? : a family's experience with Alzheimer's / by Mar-
garet Shawver ; illustrated by Jeffrey K. Bagby.
        p. cm.
    Summary: A young girl tries to understand the frustrating, frightening changes in her
grandmother caused by Alzheimer's Disease.
        ISBN 13 : 978-1-59102-174-2
        ISBN 10 : 1-59102-174-X (pbk.)

    [1. Alzheimer's Diosease—Fiction. 2. Grandmothers—Fiction. 3. Family Life—
Fiction.] I. Bagby, Jeffrey K., ill. II. Title.

PZ7.S53729Wh   1996
[Fic]—dc20

                                                                96-26730
                                                                CIP AC

Printed in the United States of America

To my own mother, who recently asked me,
"Did you have a good mother?"
I answered, "I had a *wonderful* mother."
She smiled and said, "I'm happy for you."

—Margaret Shawver

Thanks Kim, Meredith, Abigail, Caleb, Veronica, and
Shea. I couldn't have done it without you.

—Jeffrey K. Bagby

1

"She's doing it again, Mother!" Gary whispered.

"Just don't let it bother you, son," Mom shot back.

I could hear them talking while sitting at the kitchen table. I walked into the breakfast room and asked, "Are you talking about Grandma again?"

"Yes, honey, we are."

"Mom, what really *is* wrong with Grandma, anyway?"

"We're not sure, sweetie, but next week I have an appointment at the doctor's office to see if we can help her. But, I do know one thing," my mother added, looking directly at my teen-age brother, "Grandma is NOT doing this on purpose to drive you crazy."

"Okay, Mom, I get the hint," Gary responded.

I know something is wrong with Grandma, because until seven or eight months ago, my grandma had always been very independent. She used to just grab her keys and jump into the car to run errands for all the housebound friends she had. And, for forty-two years, she faithfully dashed to the car and headed out to volunteer in the mailroom every Wednesday morning at St. Anthony's Hospital. She was so proud of the fact that in all those years she had missed only six days of service to the patients in that hospital. Grandma was forever driving others to appointments, shopping, or even just out for an ice cream cone. But this disease is responsible for robbing Grandma of her freedom.

Two months ago, my parents had to take her car keys away from her. Mom and Dad even sold her car last weekend, just so she wouldn't be tempted to use it.

Grandma always drove to the beauty parlor, our church, the mall. But sometime last summer, she just could not recall how the keys worked in her car anymore. Two times last August, strangers brought Grandma home, and I remember that she seemed very confused and upset.

"Maybe she's just getting old," I mumbled to myself, as Mom left the room.

"No Ellen, it's worse than that," said Gary. "I heard Mom tell Dad last night that Grandma was getting lost on her walks around the block. It doesn't make sense. Grandma has lived in this neighborhood forever, but now nothing looks familiar to her anymore."

"What does that mean, Gary? What's happening to her?"

"You've got me. But Mom told me not to call Grandma 'nuts,' because she really isn't crazy, she just can't remember stuff like she used to."

I feel so sad about Grandma. I cry sometimes about it at night, remembering how she
used to be. She was always reading to me, or
styling my hair, or letting me give her a back rub.

Grandma used to love to brush my hair, but
she doesn't want to do it anymore. I try not to
take what she says and does personally, but it
hurts sometimes. I've known her my whole life.
I've shared my secrets with her, and we've done
so many great things together. I love Grandma.
But now she seems like a total stranger—I don't
know her anymore. I know that sounds kind of
creepy, but that's just the way I feel.

I went to lie down on the couch in the den to
do some thinking. I had to try to figure this out.
Grandma has always been good with numbers. In
fact, for years she handled all the bookkeeping for
my grandpa's clothing store. Now, she can't even
remember my Aunt Dee Dee's telephone number.

What else? Oh yeah, Grandma has ruined four whistling teakettles since she moved in with us. She would forget to fill them with water before putting them on the stove. We've been lucky Mom or Dad has always noticed it in time to stop a fire from happening. Grandma used to live out back, in our garage apartment, but Mom was afraid she'd burn the place down with one of her cooking fires. I wouldn't want Grandma to die in a house fire.

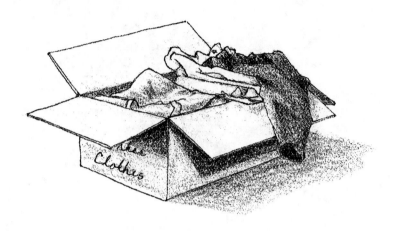

I know it's not her fault she's the way she is, but at times I get really upset—even mad—that I have to share my room with her. It's hard sometimes. My older sister, Rosemary, just moved out of the house to go into nurse's training last January, and my sister Kathleen moved out of our room and into Rosemary's old room. I *finally* had a room all to myself. Then, Grandma moved in. Now I wonder why I ever complained about sharing a room with my sister!

This sounds terrible, doesn't it? Grandma will be in bed at night and all of a sudden she'll start talking like somebody turned a faucet on in her head or something. She doesn't always talk to anyone in particular. Other times I can figure out that she's talking to her mom or dad, or Grandpa—but they've all been dead for ages! And when she does talk like that, it comes out all messed up, like someone got into her brain and scrambled up all the words. Other times, she'll start saying something and just say it over and over and over, no matter how many times I answer her. I try to help her figure out what she's trying to say, but then she gets mad at me if I do.

That's another weird thing about Grandma. She's always been this very nice person. Now, I see her moods change as fast as you can snap your fingers. She'll be real calm, like her old self, and then, from out of nowhere, she'll start crying or yelling—for no reason. Nobody knows what to do when she gets that way.

I wonder if I should tell Mom and Dad all I know about Grandma. Because we share a room, I know some things Mom doesn't know about how Grandma acts. Like last Wednesday, Mom and Dad were out on one of their date nights, and Grandma and I decided to bake cookies. I got all the ingredients out, and Grandma was able to help me mix and spoon them onto the cookie sheets. But then she stood there at the counter with the cookie sheets in her hands. She'd look at me, then she'd look around. It was like she was wondering, "Well, now what do I do?" She just didn't seem to know what we were doing or why we were doing it.

And, once I got the cookies out of the oven, Grandma swore she had never helped me make them.

"Yes, Grandma, you did. Don't you remember? We made the cookies together a few minutes ago." But I could tell by the look on her face that she had no clue. She got pretty steamed, so I just decided to drop it.

Grandma still thinks it's 1922, and she's a young girl, back in her hometown. She often speaks of her strict mother, things she did with her girlfriends, and her sweet boyfriend, Albert. She has no idea of what day it really is, or even who the president of the United States is!

How can she not know what day it is or that this is the month of July? Now, those are pretty basic things to know, don't you think?

Mom doesn't know this, but lots of nights when Grandma is sitting by herself and I'm doing my homework, she starts saying that we're in the wrong house, and we're going to get in trouble for breaking into it.

Sometimes she'll start to cry, but most of the time she just whispers it over and over again. "This isn't our house. We're in the wrong house. They're going to catch us and we'll go to jail." Each time she says it, it's like she never said it before. She has a real scared look on her face. She really does think someone is going to come to get us and drag all of us out of the house. I can tell she has no idea that she's said the same words about seventeen gillion times. It's almost like a little cog in her brain gets stuck, and it keeps spitting out the same message again and again.

Sometimes, while we are in bed at night, Grandma will tell me, "It's time to go home now, I'm tired." Her latest kick is that the FBI is coming to get us, and she has tried more than once to "escape" through our bedroom window! Maybe I should tell Mom this stuff. But my mom has seemed so stressed-out about this whole Grandma business, I hate to give her more to worry about.

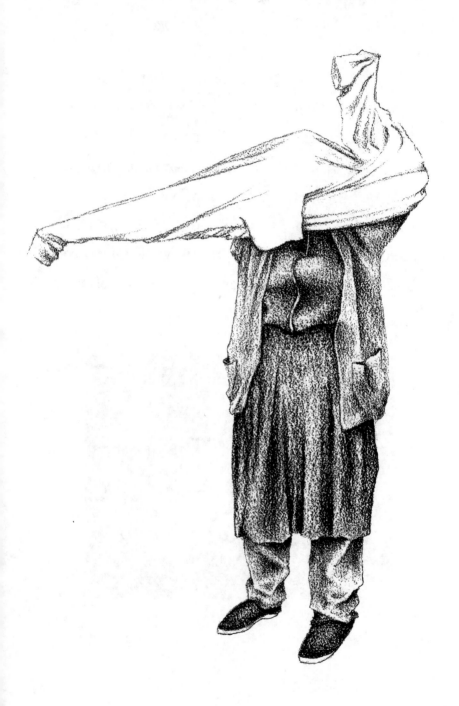

There's just so much that Mom and Dad don't know about. For one thing, they should watch Grandma get dressed! Every morning, Grandma tries to put about four or five outfits on, one on top of the other! The first time she did it, I must admit, I thought it was pretty funny. But not any more. Every day it's the same battle. She puts on one outfit after another, and I try to keep the extra outfits off of her. She gets real mad at me, but after a while, she does just keep one outfit on. At least until the next morning. This daily struggle with her makes me feel so sad.

I've also noticed that Grandma, the Great Channel Surfer of all time, now can't work the TV remote control. She gets very upset and swears she doesn't know what all the numbers on it mean! At first, I tried to explain how the remote works, but it was no use—Grandma didn't understand. Now when she gets that way, I just gently take the remote out of her hand and find something she wants to watch, without saying much. One time I kidded her and said that only us young whippersnappers could work these new-fangled electronic gadgets! She got a kick out of that.

My family is well aware of Grandma's games of hide-and-seek with everything she can stash. We still don't know where she "misplaced" two pairs of prescription glasses or three good hearing aids. But, the funniest one yet was when she put the toaster in the freezer! We all got a laugh out of that one. Of course, Grandma had no idea what we thought was so funny, but she laughed right along with us anyway.

One time, while I was eating breakfast, Grandma took a new box of garbage bags out of our pantry and, holding them up, she asked me what they were for. When I told her they were for garbage, she said, "Oh," and promptly threw them into the garbage can! I waited till she left the kitchen, then I pulled the box of plastic bags out of the bin and hid them behind the aluminum foil on a lower shelf of the pantry.

I'm sure my parents know all about Grandma's suspicious streak. Whenever she sees the small green light on our computer, the red lights on our smoke alarms, or even our little doorbell light, she's sure they are listening devices for the secret police to hear everything she says! When Grandma sees one of these lights, she drops her voice to a whisper and creases her forehead into a worried frown. Sometimes she asks us to "move to a safer room before we talk."

Gary thought up a pretty good solution to help Grandma feel safer. He placed aluminum foil over all the "listening devices," and then told Grandma that he had put up a shield to block our conversations from the secret police.

Grandma's response was so funny. She took my brother aside and whispered, "Thank goodness there's a counterspy in this house to protect us!"

If it had been anybody else who said this to Gary, he would have laughed right in their face and called them "weird" or something. But, believe it or not, he was very nice to Grandma. He said, "You just tell me if you need my services again, Grandma," and patted her on the shoulder.

Grandma used to be able to do anything. The woman had "no fear," as my mom used to say. But now, Grandma is often too afraid to leave our house, and sometimes too afraid to leave my room. She has never told us what this fear is all about. Maybe she doesn't know herself. But the look she gets on her face at those times is one of total panic. And, I feel just awful for her when that happens. When Grandma is scared about who knows what, I *don't* get much privacy in my own room!

Sometimes, when dinner is ready, Mom will call us to the table, but Grandma will just stay by herself on the couch. Gary or I will remind her that it's time to eat, but she just stares out into space as though she doesn't hear us. Then my dad will go into the living room to make Grandma get up off the couch. One time when he went to get her, she looked at him, called him Raymond (my grandpa's name), and said how very handsome he looked. My dad played along and said, "Let's go, Katherine, it's time for dinner," and the two of them walked to the table, arm in arm.

Lately, Mom has had to put the fork in Grandma's hand, and coax her to eat for the first few bites. Each time, the coaxing seems to take longer to work, and sometimes Mom has to help Grandma pick up food and put it in her mouth. What's going to happen when Mom's coaxing doesn't work anymore? Will she have to spoon-feed Grandma like she did us kids when we were babies? That will be a very difficult time for our family.

When Uncle Jack and Aunt Dee Dee came over last Sunday, Mom had to sit next to Grandma and encourage her to visit. It was almost as though she didn't remember how to talk to people. Every so often Uncle Jack or Aunt Dee Dee would say something that sparked a memory in Grandma. She'd start to talk and talk about some relative or whatever, and then she'd stop right in the middle of a sentence, or mumble something, and then she stopped talking. We all just sat there. Nobody knew what to say to her.

These things really scare me. Grandma seems to get worse as time goes by. I wish I could reach up and stop the hands of time, and my grandma could be the way she always was, before all of this started to happen.

Just this morning at the breakfast table, Grandma turned to Mom and said, "I can't remember. Did you ever get married?" Well, there was my dad, standing right next to Grandma, but I guess she didn't know who he was.

And, get this. . . last Thursday we took
Grandma to visit one of her best friends who
lives in a retirement home. As we were walking
down the hall, my grandma started introducing
me as her *sister*, and my *mom* as her *mother*! Mom
didn't say anything, but I wonder if it embar-
rassed her.

2

Mom took Grandma to the doctor today. Dad offered to take the day off from work and go with her, but Mom said she could handle it. Mom told us that the doctor she was taking Grandma to see only works on older people. She said he's a specialist in what is called geriatrics.

After thinking about it, I did finally tell Mom everything I knew about Grandma. We had a long talk the night before her doctor's appointment. I figured Mom needed to know everything I could tell her, so she could let the doctor know what Grandma was really like.

Tonight, instead of starting supper, Mom called Gary, Dad, and me to the kitchen around six, while Grandma rested on the couch. She said that the doctor told her he strongly suspects that Grandma has Alzheimer's (ALTS-high-merz) disease. It's this sickness in older people's brains. What happens is, brain cells start dying off, but the body doesn't replace them. When enough cells have died, it can start to mess up memories, how a person thinks, and even how a person behaves. I think I understand about the brain cell part. My teacher was talking in class last year about how cells make up every part of our body. I guess this Alzheimer's disease just kills off the ones in your head.

When Mom told us what the doctor said, we all agreed that that sounded a lot like what Grandma had been going through. Now all the strange things Grandma did made sense to me. She wasn't doing these things or saying weird stuff because she wanted to, but because she couldn't help herself. It was the Alzheimer's doing it. At that moment I really hated that disease.

Mom went on to tell us that at least four million Americans are afflicted with Alzheimer's disease. That's a lot of people. It is the leading cause of death among older people like Grandma.

My dad said, "I had no idea it was that common."

"But," Mom continued, "because there are more and more people who live longer in this country, the doctor says it's possible that fourteen million people could come down with this awful disease in the next fifty or sixty years!"

That made me shiver, because in fifty or sixty years, I'll be close to Grandma's age. Does that mean *I'll* get the disease? Does that mean I won't remember who I am, or that I'll forget how to feed myself? It was just too upsetting. I decided not to think about it.

Mom went on, "The doctor told me that ten percent of those people over sixty-five, and almost half of those over eighty-five, have this disease."

Personally, I think it's a rotten deal, but I didn't get a vote in the matter.

Gary asked Mom, "What causes Alzheimer's?"

"The experts don't know yet, sweetheart."

"Can Grandma be cured?" I asked. I sure hoped so.

"No Ellen, there is no cure yet." I felt like I'd been punched in the stomach.

We were all real quiet for a long while, as that news sunk in. Every one of us was crying, even my brother!

Dad asked Mom, "Why did you say the doctor 'strongly suspects' Alzheimer's? He's a doctor. Doesn't he know?"

"Because, there isn't any one test to tell a doctor for sure that it definitely is this disease. But, based on his examination of Grandma and on all the things I told him about how Grandma acts, he's about ninety percent sure that Alzheimer's disease is what is wrong with Grandma."

Then Mom looked at me and said, "Thank you, Ellen, for telling me what you knew about how your grandmother acts when your dad and I aren't nearby. You helped the doctor to come to his diagnosis. He said that what you told me will help him give Grandma medicine that can make her feel better."

Just then, Grandma walked into the room. Mom wiped away her tears, got up from the table, and made Grandma a glass of iced tea. The rest of us just sat there, glued to our seats. I felt like I had stopped breathing, but finally I gulped in a huge breath. That was the only sound any of us made while Grandma was in the kitchen.

Later that night, Mom called my sister Rosemary at nurse's school. She cried when she called Aunt Dee Dee. They talked for a long time, over an hour. Then she took a deep breath and called Uncle John in California. Mom did a lot of crying that night.

When I went into my parents' bedroom to say goodnight, my mom was lying in Daddy's arms on top of the covers. She was crying softly, and Daddy was stroking her hair. I can't ever remember a sadder day in our house, not even when our cat died.

3

It's been three months since my mom told us about Grandma's Alzheimer's. Now that we know what's happening to Grandma, it's a little easier to be around her. Each day is different. It's never dull around our house because we aren't ever quite sure what Grandma is going to do next!

Pretty much, the tears are gone, and mostly we just live each day as it comes. Sometimes I see Grandma's old sense of humor coming back, but then it always fades away. Like tonight, when we were lying in the dark of our room. I've stopped calling it "my room" because it doesn't belong to just me anymore. Grandma was trying to figure out how old she was. I asked her how old she felt.

"About twenty-seven," she answered. I could tell she was smiling.

I said, "Well, Grandma, your youngest daughter is forty-five years old!"

Without missing a beat, Grandma said, "Well then, I guess we might have a little trouble with that twenty-seven business!"

And then we laughed, I mean we really laughed, and I climbed into bed with her. And just for a moment, she held me, like she used to, when she was her "old self."